AF348358

A Day Longer

Steps towards redemption

Nnamdi Wenga Ikwuazom

Ukiyoto Publishing

All global publishing rights are held by

Ukiyoto Publishing

Published in 2022

Content Copyright © Nnamdi Wenga Ikwuazom

ISBN 9789360164942

All rights reserved.
No part of this publication may be reproduced,
transmitted, or stored in a retrieval system, in any
form by any means, electronic, mechanical,
photocopying, recording or otherwise, without the
prior permission of the publisher.

The moral rights of the author have been asserted.

This is a work of fiction. Names, characters, businesses,
places, events, locales, and incidents are either the
products of the author's imagination or used in a
fictitious manner. Any resemblance to actual persons,
living or dead, or actual events is purely coincidental.

This book is sold subject to the condition that it shall
not by way of trade or otherwise, be lent, resold, hired
out or otherwise circulated, without the publisher's
prior consent, in any form of binding or cover other
than that in which it is published.

Foreword

A proud moment to write the foreword for the book "A day longer", which is a powerful literary manuscript. A poetic endeavor to voice out the ill-practiced customs of the society. His skillful pen has meticulously described various issues such as increasing water scarcity, biodiversity and ecosystem loss, limited benefits from globalization etc. The multi angular view of the poet towards the socio cultural issues provides the reader , amusement and wisdom on the go. Nnamdi Wenga has a capability to express his feelings in less words more effectively. His poetic precision drags the mind of the reader from the first poem till the last page of the book.

The book touches the human mind when it beats to the rhythm of their heart. Being a book of high content value, A day longer is going to stay in peoples life for longer. When human mind relates, it resonates and reciprocates. The readers gets to watch the world through the poet's eyes in vivid colours. Nnamdi's book is such a polychromatic pandora filled with gems of various shades. The word usage being simple and selective, people of all levels can enjoy these poems. It is an impeccable journey where new learnings are adhered to the existing list and makes life more engaging and productive, evocating the poets muse.

In one of his poems he described the inter relationship between man and dust. The birth, strife that a human being passes through and the final victory has been illustrated with precise words. Another of his poem, "Once upon a time" as a child which sings out the narration of a life in its stages , makes each of us relatable to the poem, and this is what the success of the book , shows up. In the poem "Good night daddy", he shows his skill in expressing the poignancy etched in life situations. "At some point we are broken" is an analytical read, where the poet has dissected the phases when we meet those challenges and become strong to overpower the troubles. In a nutshell, this poetic wonder is going to be a worthiest must-have in your shelves. I would love to recommend the book A day longer as it may be an eye opener, a problem solver or a friend in solitude to find the way and move ahead.

Wishing the poet, all the success and a bright future.

Sreekala P Vijayan
Author of Soul in whole.
Admin Motivational Strips, Member of World Nations Writers Union.
Anchor of literary shows- Mighty Quills of Motivational Strips, Nuggets from the authors soul and The Voice of Mighty Quills.
Awards received :
Order of Shakespeare Medal from Motivational Strips 2021
Golden badge award from Motivational strips and Gujarat Sahithya Academy 2021
Recipient of Independence day honours from Motivational Strips and Gujarat Sahithya Academy in 2021

Dedication

To Mimi Ikpeazu (Nwanyimanarisia)

For being such a wonderful soul and for inspiring my ink.

Odua nwannem, I appreciate you.

To Onyinye Sylvia Mozie (My best friend)

For the gift of unending love, friendship and support.

Owelle nnem, I appreciate you.

To Ezennia Nonso Chukwudebe (Agadagba)

For being a pillar, friend, father and mentor.

You came into my life at the roughest of times and you have calmed my stormy waters with your patience, support, guidance and tutelage.

Nwa Aroli, I appreciate you.

To my Mother.

For being the best there is and for always believing in my dreams.

Nwa Onyido, I appreciate you.

To the Nzegwu's.

For the support and encouragement all along and for the beautiful strings of blood and love.

Ụmụ nwannem, I appreciate you.

To my woman, lover and soulmate.

For choosing to love this mad man despite being
the most beautiful, intelligent and amazing woman
of your generation. I'm yet to find perfection, but
with you, life is perfect.
Nkem, Obialunamma Wenga, I appreciate you.
To everyone of us who's going through the storms
of life.
There's more to life than bearing the tag "human"
Find your path and live like a bird.
Remember, suicide is never an option.

Contents

Candles Against The Wind

The bite hurts to deep too handle
The pain as crushing as thunderstorms
I feel my soul leave my beaten body
My eyes blind from rushing rivers gone salty
This must all be a dream
This should all be a dream

And so my heart asks again to the wind
Why do people have to die?
I know the answer to that,but then why still?
A thousand words of consolations do no aid
For my third eyes looked on hopelessly
As the reaper raided the farms before the harvest

In those thin last moments, when life slips away
What really were they thinking about?
Were they seeing the dead long gone brethren?
Or were those moments just blanks shots?

A day longer

Couldn't they feel the love in my clenching hands?
Didn't they see my resolve not to let go?

The feeling of warm bodies going cold
Would always hunt my heart forever
That feeling of helplessness as I looked on
Watching their last struggles with mortality
Each managed breath reminding me of the truth;
we're nothing but candles, helpless against the wind.

Life Happened

I once had dreams of a life
A life so perfect and comfortable
One where I would be without the ills of life
And my heart would know no breakage

But then life happened and my dreams fled
Leaving me in the stark reality of life
I saw life without it's fancy cloaks and hoods
I was torn beyond redemption

My roses turned to thorny sticks
My music lost energy and soul
I felt so rejected and lost
Each day becoming more distant

Out of nowhere, came a glitter
A watering can for my dying gardens
My hope became resurrected

4   A day longer

A beautiful morning glowed over

Now my heart has found peace
My smiles have stolen the night
The joy I feel is without fear or bounds
For my dreams though gone,still beckon knowingly.

Man And Dust

Moulded right from the dusts,
Life breathed into him.
Cursed to bear the cost of one too proud.
Blamed and judged for being as was intended,
By his own very sculptor.
Cast away from his paradise
To lead a generation of unworthy seeds
Born to suffer for no fault of theirs.

In my present state of mind, I see the flaws.
So many are they that they can't be counted,
But none of which are the faults of mankind,
For they had no role in all of this but fate;
Fate of being the ones who get to write their story,
But only to the whims of their sculptor.
So whenever I pick up the sands from the earth,
I am reminded of my beginning and my end.

The Songs Of The Night

The rains seem to be without end
As though trying to wash the sinful world
The deafening sounds upon the rooftops
Render their music to the night

On cold nights as this
The sounds of slapping flesh
And the accompanying moans and cries
Become the melodious symphony of muse

The owls roar over the hooting lions
The bats obviously have found honor and
The night becomes an orchestra of bliss
As the heavens wash all with the rains.

Once Upon A Child

Birth

First cries

Happiness in the air for new life

Suckling days

First words,though gibberish but cute

To the crawling days

Beautiful infant

The first steps unforgettable

Mother's cuddles and father's loving pecks

Early days in school

First friends and feel of the outside world

First wins and falls

Early fights and crushes

Teen years

Good and bad habits. Mostly the bad

Sin tasted so sweet and hell so nice

The first love tasted like berries

Heartbreak

Adulthood

Love comes again
More sins and definitely more hell inclined
More heartbreaks
Betrayals
Invasion and familiarity with my demons
Depression and hopelessness
Love and more heartbreaks
Critical moments and struggles with life
Hope returns
Light and positivity
Love comes singing
Redemption seems possible from here
Self realization and love for life
Gratitude and peace
Optimism

The story of this native boy,
Will always be one of fate,hope and love.
He came as a bundle of joy,
And he yet still lives as a lake of possibilities.
The waves of life though so rough,
Are but roses upon his path unto greatness.
A journey towards posterity.

Joker House Of Commotion

The people,
They suffer and sweat all for nothing
They cry out against the universe
Blaming fate for making them citizens
But yet when it's time to call the cards
They cower and scramble for peanuts
Like stray chickens on the streets
Peanuts dropped by the same villains
That they claim oppress them
How serious can they be?

The law,
For sale only to the highest bidder
Made to limit the strength of the poor man
And to set the oppressor sparkling holy
A system that favours only the wealthy
A system that bears justice but yet lacks it
Long gone are the days of the belief that the

Law was the last hope of the common man
These days,the law has become the hunter if
Not the end of the common man.

The government,
A mere father figure to cap the orgasmic
Matrimony of corruption and plundering
A bunch of manipulative charlatans draped
In flowing robes and expensive suits
But the essence of common sense flees
At the mention of their industrious names
Industrious,yes,for they represent the dedicated
Looters,killers and destroyers of the future of
The people they swore to protect and lead.

The church,
More or less houses of trade and barter
Trading your salvation for tithes and offerings
Promising heaven to the affluent who show seeds
And hell for those who chose to sow to God alone
Unholy slanderers parading in funny robes and
Adorned with soulless titles and pulpits
Draining an already suffering society in the guise

Of the Lord's name, even though it was them who
Sanctified the leaders as God-sent in the rising.

The youth,
A generation loosing focus by the seconds
Gradually getting close to being washed away
By the floods of greed, desperation and hunger
But yet still unwilling to fight the looming waves
They choose to dance with those who steal their
Futures all for sprinklings of their birthrights yet
They forever blame the government for being the
Muse for their involvement in crime and all
But they forget that nemesis knows no blames.

The educational system
Where you have to pay to be educated
And still pay to stay educated - cash or kind
A system that is lopsided to enviable heights
The aim stopped being to educate the young
It became a hustle over who sold the most books
And who got the highest grades any which way
But what do I know? Didn't I go through same?
A system that is more or less a money heist

Milking the treasury through hefty padded budgets.

The parliament,
These ones are the real jokers
Taking lesser time to pass a law prohibiting social
Media houses than it takes to pass real laws
First class comedians to the very last of the word
Bunch of uneducated educated illiterates who
Lack the barest of decorum and prestige
Embezzlers of the Divine grade and top notch
Blood suckers of the heavenly standards
Tradesmen of death,hunger and darkness.

The law enforcement,
These ones have publicly danced naked in the
Streets of shame and their butts bear no shame
Messengers of doom who do the bidding of the
High and mighty; more or less thugs in uniforms
Shooting downs the dreams of youths they were
Supposed to protect; youths who fought for them
From the barracks to the checkpoints,all I see are
Zombies who are given guns to be bought by
The highest bidder against morality.

The outcome,
A society where trust has long fled from
Religion and tribalism becoming the daily muse
A people who no longer breath the same air
The stench of intentional self degradation oozes
Countless educational institutions but yet no brains
To decipher the madness before it becomes a virus
I wonder if the early fathers could see our efforts
At becoming the mocking bird of our times or have
They hidden their faces in shame too?

Good Night Daddy

We will miss you,daddy,
But we know you're in heaven now.
We pray that you continue to guide us here,
And that you watch over us in love.

Though it's hard to believe you're gone,
Because we still feel your presence around us,
But we know you're in a better place,
Where there's neither pain not tears.

We will always remember you,
For the good memories we shared together,
And for the faith you imbibed in us.
We love you daddy.

Bringing Back Humanity

The world today is filled with bodies,
But without the sight of souls anywhere near.
A world where humans have forsaken love,
Replacing it with the quest for gratifications.

I wish for a world filled with humans who love.
A world where peace is sancrosant and revered.
I pray for a world where humanity comes first,
Before religions,class,race, colour and gender.

I wish for a world where there's no war,
No genocides, xenophobic madness and slavery.
A place where every man is equal and respected.
Not because of status but because he's human.

That world is achievable and realistic,
If only we come together as one and believe.
The world must learn that no matter what happens,
We're all the world has left; humanity.

The Life I Pray For

Some nights,I stay up awake,
Not because I'm sleepless over nothing.
Sometimes,I just want to sleep and dream
Of the life I so well desire and wish for.
A life with me and all the good things in it,
More like me being stuffed with beauty.

A life of beautiful moments and memories.
One in which my demons are denied entry,
Until at least they learn to coexist with my angels.
A life of friendship and loyalty;
One where I wouldn't have to watch my back.
A life devoid of hatred and betrayal.

I wish for beautiful daughters to call mine.
Babes who would run me over with hugs and kisses,
While their mother watches with love filled eyes.
Days by the beach with the women of my life,

Being chased adorably by the knowing waves.
Stay beautiful my babies,papa awaits you all.
A woman who I can call my pulse and soul.
One who breathes hope into my life,sending
Light flooding down my dark nights.
She'd be the one who my fears bow to.
On those days when life seems unliveable,
Her hands clasped tight in mine, would do the magic.

I don't pray for a life of excess riches,
For heavy is the heart of he who has too much.
All I need, is enough to provide for my loved ones,
And to be able to put smiles upon the sad faces
Of the hopeless and joy in the hearts of the needy.
A life dedicated towards humanity and peace.

I pray for a life where I can correct history,
By showing support and fraternising with the truth.
The truth of women being more than just women,
And the truth of women being the essence of life.
Cursed,hated and misunderstood,I would be,but
At least for once;for the right reasons.

So mine is just a simple wish; a life of love.

A life where love and not religion rules.

A life where salvation is not determined by faith.

Where equality doesn't mean marginalisation.

A life where cops wouldn't shoot innocent youths,

All because they dared to find their lost voices.

But what do I know?

A wish is all it tends to be...for now.

For I know that the days of tomorrow are close

And the moon of my beautiful wishes shall shine.

A life to call mine is all I pray for.

A life where I'm alive, and in love.

Vision 2020

The television stations,
The radio stations,
The newspapers,
No means was left out.
A glorious jamboree indeed.

The message was the same.
One preached ever so assuring in lies.
Of a nation enroute development and reform,
All of which the populace knew were scams.
A scam they had to swallow.

A change was promised, white flags of hope waved.
Sanity was promised to invade the system,
A purge of the old dirty policies of old.
It was to be the climax of the decade.
A year for radical betterment of the masses.

Vision 2020,was the word on every politician's lips.
The nation's wealth plundered to fund the campaign,
Of hope for a better country.
The message pushed as though an imminent magic
Lurking around the corner waiting for a whistle.

But the years trickled down as dry as ever,
The masses becoming impatient and bolder.
A decade of planning, advertising and promotion,
All wasted for nothing and just for what?
The height of nuisances.

Then came the deadly covid19 nightmare.
The dictators found a perfect excuse,
While the people found the perfect deaths.
The very air became toxic and unfriendly.
The world was shut in sickness and death.

Then the protests came strolling around,
The people calling for the system to be mended.
But rather than listen to the cries of the masses,
Or isn't the voice of the people God's own voice?
But they paid no heed.

Innocent youths were cut down like bushmeat.
Youths only bent on revamping their country,
All were butchered by their very own leaders,
By the same men trained to protect them.
Their blood used to paint cursed flags.

The massacre was indeed more like the change.
The one they so promised to fulfill.
This time with guns and ammunition.
Gallant youths who may have become leaders,
All gunned down in the space.

Denials and counter denials the order of the day.
The various camps busy with propaganda.
The past is called out to answer for the losses.
While the present tours the globe in audacity.
What a lovely show of patriotism.

A lovely vision for steady revamping thrown out,
Into the cold waters of politics and corruption.
The seers who prophesied the visions,
Must be so proud wherever they are,
For they have fooled themselves yet again.

And so there turned out to be no vision 2020.
Not because there was no prophet,but because
The visions were seen by blind greedy men,
With big pot bellies and bulletproof cars.
Another vision,do we earnestly await again.

Too Close

All I wanted was an extra pair of eyes

To view the beauty before me

Someone else who could help me believe she was real

I only wanted for you to breath hope into my inner doubts

To help me see how beautiful love could be

My father once said

That never should you let a man close to the source of your river

For rather than him helping you fetch the water

He'd rather stay and wash his thirst first

I pray you find my stones of guidance

Loyalty is what really matters in friendship

To the ones we claim to love

And to the ones who show us true love

There's a reason why the river never flows upwards

For broken chinaware though mended is never as good as new

A bold lizard invited to feast with the crocodiles

Should not see itself as adventurous, but rather as unfortunate

For should tempers rise over lack of meals and luck

Chaos is all that is to be expected

These are words beyond fancy cloaks and flowers

The aim of bringing friends close into the love circles

Was for them to feel the warmth I felt

To share in those happy moments that comes with friendship

But shadows would always be faster than the being it heralds

Such is the fate that befalls trust and openness

A river no matter how big, will never outmatch the ocean

What does salt have against freshwater? Nothing really

Hence the need to drink from one and sail on the other

Handshakes going beyond the elbow spells readiness for a brawl

Do you need a soothsayer to decipher my heart?

One should never go behind the tapper to question
the palm tree

About how sweet the palm wine was, that would be
ingratitude

Over fondness of another man's homestead is not a
crime

But it gets closer to sounding like call outs to the
battlefield

When it reaches a certain crescendo

No matter how friendly the snail is with the tortoise

They can never exchange their shells with each other

So is the rythm of friendship,a rythm often abused
and reduced

Many a love story have been scattered,all because at
some point

An onlooker got more involved than the wrestler in
the ring.

Dear Prompoet Buisi Mandela

Lions have always been the pride of Africa

The wolves will forever be the angels of the cold mountains

And the owls will always reign over the eagle at night

You're the child who the ancestors seek his wisdom

For a lifetime before your fathers have you been

The soul that deciphers the secrets of the divine muses

Your words,like water have no rivals nor obstacles

For you're the ocean that births the waves of poetry

A mind destined to spew the bravest of letters enroute posterity

Cease not to create the magic of your dreams

For in you has poetry found a homely bosom

In your words are the secrets of fulfillment engraved

Indeed, you're the custodian of wordsmithing.

Peaceful Storms

There's so much that my heart harbors
So much that my soul wishes to say
But I fight my very sanity just to stay longer
In some pretentious calmness and peace

Countless times have I tried to voice it out
But then I'm restrained by the voices of reason
But how long can cobwebs hold back rocks?
If the Arctic couldn't freeze down the volcanoes

Sometimes I wish I had the liberty of creation
A thousand souls wouldn't have been in existence
Maniacs posing as pious laity in St Peter's
Awaiting the said holy Padre

This anger I feel in my heart comes not from pain
But from the bliss of utter betrayal amidst love
I was fed fat on premium disloyalty

And yet still tagged the thorned rose

Unruly,I may be,but never unrelenting
For I have only come this far through acceptance
Of my flaws,scars and beautiful imperfections
I'm the sacrificial lamb who grew fangs

Even though my rage never finds anchor
I know the truth about the impending doom
For camouflage can only last so long
As can fishes never hide from the eagle.

Ongoing Longlost

A thousand times have I asked

Who I was before my mortal existence

Where was I before being born?

The early man had no clue about all that

He was content with the Stars and the sun

For to him life was a luxury he knew nothing about

We have lost touch with our roots

Seeking wisdom in unnatural ways these days

All in a bid to rediscover our origins

But sometimes fate can be funny

For how can a man who knows not his origin

Seek to know the essence of his origin?

Life is indeed a mystery.

The Mystery Of Life

What really is life?
What really is the afterlife?
What really is death?
But then I realized that we have been asking the
Wrong questions all these while
We have gotten so comfortable with living
That we never asked about the original of life

To many,life begins when we're born
From our very first cries into the world
But I beg to slander those beliefs
For I have had a taste of the forbidden fruit
Hence my rebirth in knowledgeable blasphemy
Truth they say,is life
But the mystery has only been scratched

What were we before mortality?
Where were we before our earthly arrivals?

These are the questions that we ever avoid
All because religion has termed them unholy
And has so blatantly frowned upon quests
For the hidden truths of the old ways
But I do know better than to shrink in abeyance

Countless loved ones have we lost to sleep
A sleep so ignored by we the living
A sleep we forever now to it's tentacles
Yet we still pretend to believe in eternity afterlife
Show me worse ignorance and I'll set sail to yonder
Why then do you worry about losing watch
And falling asleep someday?

If only the dead could speak to us
If only they could just whisper to our doubts
Wiping off years of fearing the unknown
Or are the ones who think they're dead?
And that they were merely just sleeping really
In some place far beyond living grasp
Confusion really is the watchword

Worry not your poor souls about the origin of life

For the answers await our condolences
And the truth may never be unearthed
Worry more about your today than yesterday
And find strength in the morning of tomorrow
For until we take that final rush of breath
Life will always remain a mystery.

Black And True

My skin seems to scream the night's glory;
Dark, mysterious and beautiful
In me,the colours have found meaning
I'm not just black by skin pigmentation,
I'm black because I'm a proud African
Born from the bellies of nature

From the mountains of east Africa
To the sahels and deserts of the horny Northside
Africa breathes nothing but life and power
Through the rivers of the western capes
Down to the southern seas and oceans
Nature really proves her point; Africa is her home

Have you seen the Maasai people of east Africa?
Have you felt the chills that accompany the drums
Of the Swahili warriors? Or the melodious singing
Of the Zulu maidens as they herald the new moon?

What about the maidens of the Yoruba people, have
You seen the power their beaded waists command?
Oh my tall Fulani damsels of the Sahara gardens
Sleek and as enchanting as they come. Behold
The prowess of the Igbo men as they till their farms
All just to provide for the shockingly gorgeous
women who grace their beds upon the moon's grace
Tell me of elegance so opulent!
None if you must know

Africa is the nesting place of the gods
My people are models of the early creations;
Spotless and built to know no evil
Her innocence however is taken for granted
Her trust taken as weakness
But one day she shall rise to rule again
For she's black and true.

Muses

They get stronger each day
Emboldened by my acceptance of life
For life itself is the window of hope
Find your muse and spin your heartbeat

Learn to listen to your soul
It sings a song every breath you take
Hold unto the vanity of paradise in your words
For in them lies your feet

Only the blind can comprehend my steps
For I choose to go with the symphony of insanity
I choose to find my lost fires and dance
This is me embracing my muse .

Stories My Father Told Me

Africa,
The land in which my fathers sowed history
The land where creation all began
From the first chants in Eden
To the early calls of the Swahili warriors
We have been here, lapping from the ovaries
Of nature and gracing the land with love

My father told me of the ancestors before him
As we sat under the complimenting moon
He told me of the wars of the old ages
How our warriors fought the toughest wars
Goosebumps of pride covered my marked skin
In pride and reverence to my heritage and lineage
I was a born warrior,sired by the gods of war

He spoke with pride about our women
I could understand the feeling surging through him

For my mother was the perfect example of Africa;
Nursing and seeing to everyone around her beam
They were the symbol of resilience and hope
Standing strong and dauntless over the times
Breathing life and love into their homes

My father stood up and moved into the courtyard
Looking straight at me,he made for me to come
I couldn't believe it! He wanted to wrestle with me
At the very first charge, he threw me to the ground
"You will get better with time" he said to me
"My father taught me how to wrestle" he continues
The pride in my chest were as loud as thunder claps

"Before the white ones came,we had our own ways"
He lit his tobacco wrap and drew in soulful puffs
"Our gods were all we had" the smoke made me cry
He saw my discomfort and smiled wickedly
"A man must never show his weakness"
He continued on about our gods and ways
The night getting even more interesting.

Rest

Tears wouldn't bring you back
For death is only but a passage
The bridge between here and there
Definitely I'll miss you a whole lot
But I'll still find strength in your name
I'm grateful for the times we spent together
I'm inspired by your legacies
And your memories will live forever in my heart
I'll let the world know how amazing you were
How big a supporter of hardwork you were
I'll sing your praises to my unborn children
Reminding myself and us all of your love
I'll miss you,yes,but every actor takes a bow
Every Rose has a thorn
And every season has an end
Rest in peace,dear father.

Once Upon My Heart

It was once colourful and lovely
Like the fields in springtime
It once knew the world as home
But only for just sometime
Darkness was it's destiny and fate

Poor thing oh my goodness
Shut out against the universe
Left to die from the cold harsh world
A world it so much believed in
A world so Savage and undeserving

Stormy nights and brave mornings
Through the waves of hurts and calamities
It always came bouncing back stronger
Taking the pains as though meant to be
Like Christmas even in a hurricane

Subdued by love countless times
Broken and left to rot a million lifetimes
A lesson learnt from each fall in grace
A will still so strong and dauntless
Never for a second judging the world

Gratitude is all it carries amidst all
A few drops of tears no doubt
But hopeful still yet
That someday colours will return
And it may then find cause to fly again.

Solicitude

The love we share amounts to nothing
If our hearts do not go beyond just words
Beyond just holding hands and kisses
Solicitude is what makes love thicker.

What is love without sacrifice?
It's like trees growing without roots
Like flowers without petals
And like life, without death

A million times I'd still love to love you
But that only depends on the next few breaths
That's just how complicated life gets to be
Each step determining the whole journey

Love is beyond the sweet poems and songs
It's more than just sweet moans upon thrusts
Love grows roses upon rocks far in the deserts

It has no sides,only but just perspectives

If only love had a face,a name and a home
Mankind wouldn't be close to it
For what use is a love without denial and pain?
Love is bold only from solicitude.

Sleep, Dear Father

A thousand words I wish to say
To tell you how amazing you were
To sing your praises as usual
But words fail me without shame

A worthy life you lived till the end
Serving your maker with such diligence
Putting sincerity before worldly pleasures
The perfect example of a devoted believer

At home you were the most caring husband
And the world's best father and friend
Creating a family so strong in love and unity
You remain the head still yet

A supporter of hardwork and perseverance
You encouraged and motivated your children
To go beyond boundaries and stereotypes

Making them achieve greater heights in life

Death is never the end of life rather the beginning
Of a new life on the other side with the maker
A place where pain and worries do not exist
Where finally you can rest indeed

I'll be the man you've always wanted in us
Holding onto your memories and words
Sleep dear father,for one day when we're old
And fulfilled,we shall meet to part no more.

People

Some were terribly horrible
Others were just wonderful and blessed
Talk about the good, bad and the ugly
I've met them all
I might even be one of yours too

I've had days when I felt mankind was a curse
On other days I've also loved beyond words
Creating memories worthy of eternity
I've had my fair share of controversies
For I'm ever seriously unserious

People are more than you can ever imagine
I think we all need to appreciate ourselves more
This life is never easy, wasn't even meant to be
So rather than focus on the flaws of people
Let's hold dear the good memories we shared.

I Am

I am the rains that waters the desert
Sending the storms into exile

I am the son of my fathers
Proof that my ancestors were legendary

I am the air that sustains creativity
Birthing art so pure and rare

I am the offspring of deities so strong
Ojedi and ogiliya, I salute thee

I am the joy of my mother and her mothers
The mighty iroko of her womanhood

I am the soil that nurtures the grains of hope
So fertile the harvest is endless

I am the ancient kings of my land reincarnated
My bloodline so pure and blue
I am the fire of resilience,ever burning alive
Unbreakable by the forces of despair

I am the bearer of love for my woman
Her anchor through the waters of love

I am he that was before the invasions of cultures
The very last of the old ways and religions

I am the salt that favours the oceans
The last of the water gods

I am the embodiment of history and heritage
Draped in the tongues of my fathers

I am the perfect example of godliness
Moulded to sparkling imperfection

I am a seeker of forbidden knowledge
Destined for the shores of posterity

I am he that draws moans from the maidens
Gifting them ecstasy so high and blissful
I am the one who has lost all fear of death
For I have found peace in my heart

I am the son of Africa in flesh and blood
The creator of my paths.

Odogwunnam

The sun seems to have gone on exile
And the moon seems afraid of the night now
I look up only to find the stars missing
The rains have also fled from my side
Leaving me hopeless and so lonely

Every man has his birth and still his death
It's all the flaws of humanity and mortality
I know I should embrace the harsh reality
And accept it as the will of our creator
But I beg to hold unto my tears

I remember the love that sparked in your eyes
You were the perfect example of fatherhood
Guiding our very steps with godliness and care
Your love had no rival and your heart no evil
You were the real African man

The world expects me to man up and be brave
But I feel more like bats hanging in a cave
Upside down and confused beyond words
For losing you was like losing sight
You were my strength and courage against life

In all my steps in life, you always supported me
Reminding me of the virtues of hard work
You showed the seed of faith in me steadfastly
Always pointing out that God was the only way
You were the example of a prayerful father

I know my tears won't bring you back
But I find solace knowing you're up there
By the right hand side of the creator of all life
Looking down and smiling at we below
Forever being our unseen fortress and guide

I love you my dearest father
To the world you're gone,but I know better
For you've gone to be at rest after a worthy life
I pray you continue to hover over us with love
You're forever in my heart, odogwu nnam.

The Poet And His Muse

Theirs is a love so uncommon
For even without speaking,they say a million words
Words,paper,ink and the poet; a perfect family
The world may see the poet as just any other
But few or none actually see his muse

A poet writes but only as long as his muse wills
Just like a car and petrol
His muse is the bed of his magic and spice
And to it alone does he pay homage to
It's okay if you're lost at this point

The mind of a poet is one so sincere and dedicated
For he carries the burden of life and hope
Creating words that rhyme to the frail hearts
Caressing and tending to broken souls and
Still remaining mortal but pristine

A poet is god over his creation
But his muse wills his magic wand
More like the unseen hand in a card game
Theirs is really the perfect love story
Filled with ageless love and peace.

Unclean Water

I'm on a path of self discovery
Climbing up the hills of theories
Swimming through the waters of confusions
All in a bid to atone for my ignorance

 Yes, ignorance
For I've been fed fat on lies all life long
Lies of religion being the only way to peace
And lies of me being a sinner

I'm like the waters of Africa; muddy but proud
My heart knows neither hate or trust
For the music of hope is one too rigorous
And so I dwell in the irony of fate

I'm neither holy not unclean
More or less a better version of freedom
For I've unlearned all man was supposed to be

To become the best of my choices

Permit my refund of early knowledge
For I chose to be ignorant of love
But I remain the same time and season
The very best of unclean waters.

Unarmed Soldier

A thousand words piercing through my heart
Words that came from a place of hurt and denial
I died a thousand times over again
Each time feeling better than the other
But I live to tell the story
Of a boy who loved and a girl who believed
Love is the greatest soldier
Armed with nothing but emotions
Love is the ultimate weapon of war
Unarmed but deadly still yet.

If I Were To Meet God

Sometimes I wonder how we got here
How did mankind find their way here
I wonder who hung the skies up there
The sun shines through a million miles
And yet it never hurts the stars or the moon
I tried to find answers from the holy places
But I was called unclean and a lost soul
All because my soul got free of it's chains

Images of the creator : aren't we supposed to be?
But man is the architect of mortal destruction
A being filled with envy, greed and lust
I beg to slander the holy doctrines of old
But wasn't it man who invented wars?
Oh, I remember. Wars were fought up above
Long before mankind were even created
A splitting image of their creator indeed

So if I happened to find God somewhere
I'll ask him for just one favour; one big enough
That he take a walk with me down earth
That he leaves behind his angels for the moment
I'll need us to walk alongside nothingness
Or how else can he be able to experience
The pleasure of our exclusive excursion
A walk down history and creation

We'd first visit the garden of Eden against time
I need to know what really happened there
Why he allowed the serpent tempt eve
And why he allowed Adam to fall for the bait
Which father watches his children fall into harm
And still comes by to punish their ignorance?
Well, we all know who did and who still does
An amazing thing, don't you think?

I'll need to know why he allowed the devil roam
Why he didn't just cage him up in hell; if any be
Who sends down a multitude of betrayed demons
To dwell amongst his children? Absolutely nobody
I need to look into his eyes and see his soul

I need to understand what our options were
How we were supposed to outmatch them
Flesh up against holy monsters. Oh my goodness

He should explain why he made Solomon the best
Why David was the one after his heart
But yet I'm a sinner for even smaller sins
Or is it just me smelling partiality and compromise
Something I know so well he possesses
But yet condemns us for having
Like it was us who chose to be in this world
Perfect images we are indeed

Hitler , Stalin and Constantine were all born
I need to know why he allowed that to happen
I was told , or rather he said he knows even in
Our mothers womb who/what each shall be
Why then didn't he just stop evil from being born?
Or was it also to test our faith in his glory?
Or was it just plain egoism and inability to
Admit that at some point,he failed us?

He sees the world of today and tomorrow even

I need to know why we pay for sins long before us
I need to know why man's heart is so bitter
I know he sees the wars and tribulations of today
But do we really expect him to intervene?
He also saw the calamities of yesterday, remember
Nations up against nations and children dying
Children who you asked that we be like

I need to know why death and sickness exist
Why hunger and thirst have killed forever
Why inequality is the basis of our very lives
Obviously he saw all of this world
Even before he created this world, right?
What do I know? He made us so he alone knows
Why we are so evil and yet so loud in faith
This madness is so sane

Does hell really appreciate our very best?
For it's said that no rich man can make heaven
But he's a wealthy God, isn't he?
Or maybe he just doesn't want competition
Oh,yea! He said something like that actually
Why keep hell when we are only pawns here?

Why save few and leave the others?
Aren't they all supposed to be your children?
He came for the sinners but yet condemns us
Casting us away to be devoured by his mistake
Why are some saved and others not?
What the hell is grace? If not plain rigging
This time of conscience and fate
Don't we all deserve to be happy and prosperous?
Aren't we all supposed to be healthy?
So why all the flaws in salvation?

Why did he allow diseases and disorders to exist?
A world constantly changing and killing us
Climate change, natural disasters and worse
Signs of the last days he called them
I can only imagine the first days indeed
But again, what do I know?
Images, I repeat images, are we
Sculpted to draping imperfection

I want him to know that I don't plan on heaven
That I have found peace with my sins here
And that whenever the trumpet sounds

It will only be taken for the music it should be
Because in all our history according to the book
We are images of our father; images of him alone
Let him who be without holiness cast a stone
For replicas of heaven have we always been.

At Some Point, We All Got Broken

Life,
We never chose to be born into this world
Neither did we chose our race and colour
Somewhere obviously and hopefully better
Were we before we found our way down here
Aren't we all victims or should I say,pawns?
For we live in a world predestined to fail
A world where today is dwarfed by the future

Love,
We never chose who to love or hate
Fate decided that and all we did was follow
A life of heartbreaks,denial and deception
I broke a few hearts in my search for love
I ruined friendships worthy of being family
All just in a bid to find that special someone
How can I atone for sins beyond words?

Faith,

Allow me to turn a blind eye to religion

For all I see amongst the brethren

Is nothing but organized confusions

A systematic colonization of choices

People being peacefully forced to believe

In a being who has no origin nor forgiveness

I beg to avoid this purge

Conscience,

I had one a long time ago but then life happened

I was made to see the butterflies for the hawks

That they obviously were; what a life

I betrayed trusts and I also got served

Nowadays I just shut my heart and breathe

For what use is a light in the wake of the storm?

And so I allow life to drown my inner eyes

Redemption,

A lady once loved me beyond words

So willing to walk alongside my soul

But then they came; my demons and kinsmen

Yes so, because I know them by their winds
I know my flaws are way to many; beautiful too
For weren't demons angels before the stories?
Still I seek to payoff my darkness and sins

Hope,
Something the sinner looks up too
Something I look up too
Hush, can you hear the rivers flowing?
You can't, because you've lost your route
Forsaking the spittle of your forefathers
And embracing vain righteousness
Do I hope to hope? Pardon my ignorance

Acceptance,
Arms open to embrace my sins beyond words
For I'm only but a man who lost his sight
A man whose feet found speed before suckling
I see the seeds of my shadows lurking around
Waiting for water and light to grow so big
Big enough to uproot my sanity and peace
But can one deny his choices only after truth?

I know I deserve nothing but pain reinforced
I know I've been the best of evil and sin
But brave your eyes and cast your stones
The truth lies not so far away
A victim is all I am and will always be
For I'm only a mirror in contest with reality
I remember the faint taste of love and I smile
For at some point, we all got broken.

Songs For When I'm Gone

A man has his time of birth and death
Time to cry and time to smile
So why shy away from the harshness of truth,
That one day we all shall die ?
Why try so hard to believe in forever?

The birds my fathers saw are all gone
The farms they worked on are now cities
Even Methuselah had to take a bow sometime
So why pray that you live without the joy of end
When yet you believe in the afterlife

Mourn me not more than you would spilled milk
Shame be unto they that cry longer than the sun
Why hold unto the vanity of eternity
When the dreams of today lie unattended to?
Would that not be foolishness in royal garments?

When I'm old and then long gone to sleep
When I'm without pain,noise and faith
Do not waste your soulless tears for me
Soulless yes,for would you rather join me?
We know you know better than to nod your head

Do not litter my graveside with wreaths or tears
Rather feed me daily with the best of delicacies
Pay double for the best palmwine and gin
Don't forget to add the African salad and snuff
Pay the Piper to play our native war tunes

Reminisce about the maidens we conquered
Laugh over the escapades of our youth and
Hiss at the names of men who betrayed us
But never for once cry over the men who died
For the dead abhor such foolishness

Beat your chests in pride and wrestle to my name
In honour to my memories and not for hate
Laugh about the clumsiness of the women
And talk about my works and escapades we shared
Over mouthfuls of dry bushmeat and palmwine

Talk about the bond we shared with pride
Waste not a single tear over my headstone if any
Laugh,love and toast to my songs of hope
Pen the best of words and read aloud to me
For life is the indeed the greatest of all muses.

Children Of Wartorn Africa

We're the children of Africa
Children of the blessed continent
Our lands knew peace before the invasions
Our fathers stayed home and tilled the farms
Our mothers were alive to nurse our hearts
All this ended with the invasions

First they came as tradesmen
Offering peace and selling fancy vanities
Then they came as the righteous brothers
Selling this time a different religion and gods
But pretence can only last so long
They were invaders camouflaged as doves

They soon had their way with our rulers
Fooling them with the fancy gifts they brought
Soon they acquired grounds for infiltration
Convincing our rulers to abandon their gods

They soon conquered our holy places
Burning them down to the grounds
We became a people without gods

Then came the casting away of the sheep skin
And we saw the wolves that they truly were
We became hunted in our very own lands
Bundled off as slaves to lands unknown
Their holy books stuffed down our throats
And their gods replacing our gods in audacity

We found our way back centuries later
But the scars are never to heal completely
A child never forgets the taste of fire
Our hearts still nurse the grievance of betrayal
For it was our very own who betrayed us
All just for pieces of silver and fancy clothes

Africa of today may seem peaceful
But the truth hides away far from that notion
We're bleeding from wounds so deep and severe
The wounds of internal poisoning
Brothers killing brothers and kingdoms falling

This time we are our own invaders

From the Cape of madiba's motherland to
The valleys of zik's fatherland, war tunes abound
Civil wars,genocides, xenophobic madness, tribal
wars and religious intolerance have become norm
The seed of the early invaders finding new life
As we colour our rivers with our own blood

Fathers going off to fight another man's war
Mothers being raped alongside their daughters
By the very men who should protect them
The chaos is deafening and the ovation loud
Children becoming orphans at alarming rate
The world watches as Africa burns itself down

We shall rise again as long the sun shines
But only if we're alive to see the sun
We're the children of war torn Africa
Battered by our very own soil and spirits
We pray for the world to hear our story
And for us to create a better story by ourselves.

(34) EVERY LION WAS ONCE A CUB
Like the great ojadili of old fame
I tred the earth in dominant steps
Defiant of the worries and vanity of the world
I am he who was long favoured before his birth
A king chosen to rule even before his father's
Like the iroko tree my roots go way beyond
The comprehension of mortal minds

I am the cub who drove the wolves away
With nothing but smiles and my innocence
A child of destiny who shall break records
Shattering the halls of history to build my empire
I am the herb that cures the ills of life
I stand tall before the mirrors of tomorrow
To admire the king I see before me

I am her jewel and shelter
I am the key to her longetivity
For in my eyes are the keys to her heart hidden
However rough the seas of life may be
I am forever her anchor and lifeboat

I am a child of destiny not circumstance
The lion who shall rule his pride forever.

Let It Go

How much longer will you carry your burden?
Look beyond your expectations and just live
For no matter how much you worry about your life,
Fate will always have it's way,so let it go.

(36) A MESSAGE FOR OUR ANCESTORS
(The political imbalance of the Nigerian system)

The sky has lost it's blue to bloody red
Beautiful waters turning red at light speed
Don't ask me for explanations or pointers
The aroma of doom cascades the air defiantly.

What clouded your judgements?
Was it the ecstatic feelings of false freedom?
Or the laughable hopes for a greater tomorrow?
Tell me, what really were you thinking?.

Cats and dogs will never find conference without it being fiction

The mouse and the cat too, I can go on listing obvious disasters

Whoever told you that the southern sun could romance

With the northern star? Or were you just plain gullible?.

The colonial slave masters we love to blame

But it was you who fell for their cheap thrills and spins

A closer look would have exposed their cheap lies

And a little poke would have bared their fancy robes.

The southern cape breathes a different air in surviving

The northern sahel was born for it's own spine

So why the abominable matrimony?

A union built to fail right from it's very inception.

Wars, genocides, murders and political dehumanization

What fate has the southern cape not been fed fat on?

But yet her sun shines daringly beyond the horizons

Sending her rays far into the world.

I wish you were here today to witness this morning of growth

To see how much love flows uncontrollably from north to south

You should see cattle till the farms of the wealthy peasants

The scale of love and peace is shockingly amazing.

I spit, but not at the devil, for even he knows of better compromise

The mess of today originated from sheer greed and sentiments

Pitting water and ice in winter and expecting warmth against the cold

Tell me of better foolishness and i'll show you heaven.

Youths get slaughtered like beef, but wait, isn't it expected?

Especially since cattle is worth more than lives of some people

Herders by day and bandits by night. Did I just say bandits?

for a moment, I thought I sounded like the present leaders.

Clueless, that what we've become. Losing common sense by the day

Tribalism and religion suddenly finding prominence

The marginalized becoming shooting games for the invaders

What a fanfare of bitterness and ungodliness.

I hope you see this morning that has befallen us

I hope you see the beautiful darkness you've sentenced us to

Rest on dear fathers gone, the rain shall wash us all as you dreamed

But before then, we shall dig up your bones with our ink and tears.

About the Author

Nnamdi

Nnamdi is a young poet from the beautiful city of Ọnịcha (Onitsha).He writes for his voice to be heard and for his soul to sleep in the memories of yesterday.

Nnamdi is an internationally renowned poet and his books and poems have been critically acclaimed.

www.ingramcontent.com/pod-product-compliance
Lightning Source LLC
LaVergne TN
LVHW041736190726
843493LV00008B/2369